Tabl

- Federal Acquisition Regulation (FAR) Complaints

- Waste, Fraud and Abuse Reports (medical errors, contamination, espionage, etc.)

- Prohibited Personnel Practices (discrimination, black-balling, privacy, etc)

- Office of Special Counsel (OSC) and Merits System Protection Board (MSPB) Cases

- Inspector General (IG) and other Investigations

- Veterans and Survivor Benefits Denials & Medicare/Medicaid Fraud

- Workplace Harassment & Violence/Suicide Prevention

Goals and Objectives:

- Engage peers in resilience case management, outreach, and networking opportunities

- Define whistleblowers as the first relators of wrongdoing with psychosocial impacts like First Responders who also protect the public welfare and individuals from harm

- Mediate between employees and employers to resolve issues

- Offer education and training curriculums in managing and responding to workplace conflicts/abuses, leadership development, resilience, and diversity and inclusion

- Engage media in a whistleblower public advocacy campaign

- Inform Congress on areas of needed reform and case consultation

Introduction – My Story

Whistleblowers of America (WoA), like many organizations before it, was born out of personal experience. In 2015, "whistleblower retaliation" were just words to me. Then, the puzzle pieces of my career's demise began to come together.

I had been appointed by the Obama Administration to the Department of Defense (DoD) to work in the office of the Under Secretary of Defense for Personnel and Readiness (P&R). I had been professional staff at the House Veterans Affairs' Committee when a member of the President's National Security Council asked me to come to DoD. I said no. But when the White House Personnel Office called to vet me, I thought, "you go where you are led." My boss on the Hill and Members of Congress were thrilled that I had been asked to join "the historic Obama White House" and I entered the Administration full of hope and promise.

Unfortunately, P&R experienced a great deal of turmoil and transition during the next 8 years. We would see ten P&R Under Secretaries come and go during my tenure at DoD. It also meant that I directly reported to 12 different supervisors and moved offices 15 times. Even though it was chaotic, I was proud to have worked on disability policies impacting wounded warriors, mental health care accessibility for the National Guard and Reserves, suicide prevention, and diversity and inclusion. But, my whistleblowing story began in 2011, after I founded the Defense Suicide Prevention Office (DSPO). The new office oversaw suicide prevention and resilience policy and programs across the Services. I created all the initial job descriptions and secured appropriated funds from Congress. We wrote new policies, provided oversight, evaluated programs, instituted new approaches to peer support, targeted specific risk factors using predictive analytics, and improved data and surveillance reporting. We were seeing successes and the military suicide rate was trending downward. I received several awards for my work, including recognition from then Defense Secretary Hagel and two external organizations.

In the summer of 2013, a new Deputy Assistant Secretary came to DoD from a private contracting firm where she had been vice president and her husband a subcontractor. When I refused to fund her former company and reported my perception of her conflicts of interests to her supervisor, I thought I was following DoD professional ethics training. However, I believe she retaliated by obstructing my ability to compete for the DSPO director position that I had created and held for 3 years when it was converted from a political to a career position. She chaired the Executive Evaluation Panel and "decided" I was not qualified. When I figured out that she was involved in the process, I felt she could not have been "fair and objective" as regulations require based on her previous animus towards me that others willingly documented. So, I filed complaints with the Office of Special Counsel (OSC) and the Office of Inspector General (IG) at DoD and Department of Veterans Affairs (VA) for contract fraud, whistleblower retaliation, and prohibited personnel practices (all with the help of a human resources specialist since I didn't even know what those terms meant at the time). To make matters even worse, discovery revealed a pre-existing friendship between my retaliator and the person selected for the job. Emails showed that she was encouraging that person to apply. She did not encourage me to apply. In my view, this was pre-selection and favoritism and was not based solely on candidate qualifications as the law outlines.

As I write this, it is three years later, and these cases are still under review and investigation. During the intervening years, I endured an attempt to give me a lower performance evaluation and an accusation of misspending funds, both which I refuted and won. I found myself in marginalized roles and assignments and moved to more meager spaces that were not comparable to other employees of equal rank. I had my memory of events questioned by superiors and investigators and my integrity impugned. I became tainted by leadership who just wanted me to leave and as a result became ostracized by others who did not want to get involved. I had to answer, "What happened?" questions from sympathetic coworkers discrimination can occur. *Toxic Tactics* can take on several forms that whistleblowers are not prepared to recognize or deal with. In its 2017 national survey, the Workplace Bullying Institute found that 19 percent of American workers reported being bullied while on the job, another 19 percent witnessed it, 61 percent were aware of it, and 29 percent of those targeted were silent about it.[12]

Unfortunately, since most whistleblowers do not perceive their initial disclosure as whistleblowing, they have not consulted the law to know what their responsibilities or protections are and to whom they should make their disclosure. There are laws that apply to federal, state, and local governments and the private sector with nuances for employees or others who "relate" the wrongdoing. (See Appendix D on Whistleblowers and the Law)

Before Blowing the Whistle: What is Your Strategic Plan?

(To complete your full Strategic Plan, see Appendix C):

Important questions to ask yourself or your mentee before making any disclosures are:

- Is this my opinion or do I have factual proof?

- Am I being bullied, harassed, or is this a personality conflict?

- What is your proof? (documents, reports, charts, letters, emails, studies, recording, etc.)

- Can you legally obtain proof? (You can't break into the boss' office and steal proof or remove documents from the office that are not allowed to be removed. You can record a conversation you are a party to, but you <u>cannot</u> hide a device and record others.)

- Am I being insubordinate?

---

[12] Namie, G. Workplace Bullying Institute. Workplace Bullying Survey, June 2017. http://www.workplacebullying.org/wbiresearch/wbi-2017-survey/. Accessed: Jan 15, 2018

- What is my role in the problem and its solution? Am I hearing feedback?

- Is the information proprietary, private, confidential, or classified?

- Did you sign a non-disclosure agreement when you were hired? What are its limitations?

- What does your employee handbook say about handling organizational information and using its computers, fax machines, and phones?

- Can you whistle blow on your own time with your own resources? (Hint – answer should be yes.)

- Are there other employees who will support you? Will they submit written statements?

- Did you discuss this with family? Are they prepared for what this might bring or the time it could take for a resolution?

- Who else will support you? Union? Colleagues? Organizations? Media? Congress?

- What laws, regulations or policies protect your disclosure?

- Can your disclosure be made confidentially or anonymously for whistleblower protection?

- Do you need your own attorney? How will you afford those costs?

Who Do You Tell?

Knowing who to tell is critical to your success. This is the next set of important questions to consider before doing anything else. Depending on the circumstances and the legal protections afforded by the nature of the disclosure, it is sometimes better to use one source for disclosing versus another. If you believe your issue can be resolved by your organization in an expeditious and fair way, then consider using your chain of command or an internal source. If the proprietary, private, confidential or secret information. The media is not a protected disclosure and you should be mindful not to be slanderous or libelous when talking to reports or writing an opposite the editorial page (op-ed) to express your opinion. Defaming someone else can get you in trouble. Bona fide reporters will want evidence, so make sure that what you share with the press was legally obtained.

Is Mediation Right for You?

Once you have decided what to disclose and who to tell, you should be ready to negotiate a desired outcome. Under the law, agencies are required to have a policy on Alternative Dispute Resolution (ADR) to help mediate and make conflict resolution decisions. An ADR can include conciliation, cooperative problem-solving, dispute panels, facilitation, fact finding, interest-based problem solving, bargaining, settlement conferences, ombudsman representation, peer review, and alternative discipline. An ADR is a more informal process that does not need to go before a judge, so a quicker (less costly) resolution can be reached. However, mediators and facilitators do not have decision making authority. According to OPM, any ADR should involve a neutral, impartial individual as a mediator/arbitrator in resolving the dispute.[18] This could be an Ombudsman or an EAP counselor. A facilitator may be used from outside of the organization, such as services offered by the FMCS. For example, a struggling employee who has reported disability discrimination and harassment might be better assisted if reasonable accommodations could be made with a referral to CAPTEC (see Resource Guide under DoD). This independent evaluation would provide options to mangers to support an employee and de-escalate hostilities.

Each party should agree on that person or those panel members. When a panel is used, it should consist of employees and managers who

---

[18] OPM Alternative Dispute Resolution Handbook. https://www.opm.gov/policy-data-oversight/employee-relations/employee-rights-appeals/alternative-dispute-resolution/handbook.pdf. Accessed: February 8, 2018.

volunteer for this duty and who are trained in listening, questioning, and problem-solving skills as well as the specific policies and guidelines of the panel. Peer review panels may be a standing group or created ad hoc to address employee disputes depending upon the circumstances, but should meet criteria related to fairness, objectivity, and when necessary, have technical knowledge, such as when a dispute involves medical standards for patient care. The agency should be able to provide a list of arbitrators for the parties to choose from.

When issues are less contentious, and conciliation is the goal, then the mediator helps develop agreements for conditions and facts that need to be addressed. A mediator can help problem-solve when the challenge is less polarizing and there is a mutual concern to be addressed. In some cases, simply brainstorming solutions together can resolve the disagreement. A mediator may meet with each party individually and/or jointly. Non-binding arbitration helps parties identify labor agreements that can later be made binding.

When issues are more contentious than a mediated arbitration is more likely warranted, whereby two outside parties are utilized. One party mediates and the other arbitrates any remaining issues that the mediation cannot resolve. This approach reduces the complexity of the mediation and allows for the arbitrator to be impartial when making a binding decision.

A minitrial is another approach to resolve highly charged issues between management and employee. It is a structured settlement process in which each party presents summaries of their cases in front of major decision makers who have the authority to settle the dispute. It is not as formal as court proceedings, but the decision-maker usually has a legal background.

Getting a third-party opinion can help establish parameters and facts. An early neutral evaluation that is non-binding can be obtained if facts or data are in question. This information can be submitted in court and can be used instead of more expensive forms of discovery, such as depositions. A similar approach to an evaluation is fact-finding. This allows for a non-binding situational assessment and potential resolution recommendations.

Understanding Whistleblower Retaliation

Once wrongdoing is identified and a protected disclosure is made, *Toxic Tactics* may be used by corrupt or insecure managers to avoid or diminish the nature of the allegations or impugn the credibility of the whistleblower. These tactics often occur in clusters and are not mutually exclusive. Often, they are insidious and often hard to prove. Although these tactics may be unethical and toxic for the organization itself, they are not necessarily illegal, except where legally protected classes of employees are involved, whistleblower retaliation laws were violated, or court decisions can be cited.

However, it is important for whistleblowers (along with their families, mental health providers and lawyers) to understand the taxonomy of retaliation and the *Toxic Tactics* employed so that they can give language to what is happening to them and understand it, and perhaps make a case for damage remuneration for pain and suffering. Whistleblowers and the professionals that assist them need to know that this is a real phenomenon. For example, during the Nixon Administration, the *Malek Manual* was produced by the White House as a guide for removing "unwanted" civil servants from government using these types of Machiavellian tactics.[19] These tactics have remained persistent and morphed from Administration to Administration.

Today, within the military, there is a body of knowledge that identifies characteristics of toxic command climates. Yet, these manipulative and disingenuous leadership behaviors reign because they often are so deceptive and overwhelming. Plus, in environments that tolerate toxicities, commanders who use them can become very successful. Toxic leadership can fall under the radar screen because senior civilian or military leaders do not see or hear from the more junior personnel experiencing it. Senior leaders only see or hear about the achievements of the commander/manager, not their abuses because junior enlisted or lower-ranking officers fear retaliation and do not was to be perceived as disloyal to their teams or unable to

---

[19] Devine, T., Maassarani, T.F. (2011) The Corporate Whistleblower's Survival Guide. Berrett-Koehler Publishers. San Francisco. 19-20.

handle their missions.[20] They learn to "suck it up" or to "go along to get along" as the sayings go. There is even a level of pride within the military ranks to have "toughed it out." Unfortunately, those troops who find unethical behavior aberrant and speak up are often labeled as "crybabies" and seen as not able to "man up" and retaliation for not doing so is severe. Bad situations are referred to as "embracing the suck."

Although accounts of military sexual assault or harassment have decreased from 2014 to 2016 reports,[21]military women who reported being victimized, also have found themselves to be the ones who have had their careers impacted more than the perpetrators. Therefore, regardless of how horrendous the crime or the level of humiliation and betrayal, many Service members (women and men) do not report the crime for fear of the professional and personal repercussions. Victims are often the ones who are reassigned or detailed to other locations, not the perpetrators. Nonetheless, depending on, if and how these crimes are reported, the ability to access benefits and health care in the future will be affected. For example, if a female sergeant does not report being sexually assaulted by the captain that she serves under for fear of retaliation and further harassment, when it comes time to apply for VA benefits for PTSD, she has no proof of Military Sexual Trauma (MST)[22] unless she can prove with other documentation (performance evaluations, witness statements, etc.) that her MST occurred. The #METOO movement[23] is indicative of how widespread sexual harassment in the workplace can really be.

In the literature on the Holocaust and other difficult to discuss traumas, this phenomenon is often labeled "the conspiracy of

---

[20] Reed, G.E., (2015) Tarnished: Toxic Leadership in the U.S. Military. Potomac Books. University of Nebraska Press. 10-18.
[21] Department of Defense, Sexual Assault Prevention and Response Office. Accessed January 6, 2018:
http://www.sapr.mil/public/docs/reports/FY16_Annual/FY16_SAPRO_Annual_Report.pdf
[22] MST is a term unique to VA and codified in 38 U.S.C.
[23] Sexual Harassment, #METOO. https://metoomvmt.org/

silence."[24] In these toxic environments, it is taboo to speak out, so very few do. Other toxic tactics (discussed below) that offer the false comfort of group cohesion and unit loyalty become the breeding-ground that justifies silencing the victim(s). This becomes a vicious cycle of organizational dysfunction that enables bad leaders to be promoted and forces good troops to leave military service.

Toxic Tactics of Management Retaliation

Dysfunctional environments allow for whistleblower retaliation and workplace bullying and harassment., which perpetuates a culture for wrongdoing. Based on this author's work with whistleblowers, the following tactics have been identified as unique paradigms, which taken together form a Whistleblower Retaliation Checklist©.[25]

Case examples are given with whistleblower identities disguised and their names changed to protect privacy and confidentiality. Tips are offered to assist with identifying and dealing with each of these tactics. Having a taxonomy for these mistreatments helps whistleblowers understand what they are up against and validates their experiences. It can also be used to inform clinical and legal teams responsible for helping the whistleblower recover. These tactics do not occur in any order or in isolation of each other. They are often used in conglomeration by poor managers to silence or discredit the whistleblower and separate them from anyone else who might share their same sense of ethical dissonance.

Gaslighting – This tactic takes the form of diminishing or questioning the legitimacy of the wrongdoing disclosed or the whistleblower's memory or perception of events. The term is derived from the 1944 movie,

Figure 5: 1944 Gaslight movie poster

[24] Danieli, Yael. (1984). Psychotherapist's participation on the conspiracy of silence about the Holocaust. Psychoanalytic Psychology. 1. 23-42. 10.1037/0736-9735.1.1.23.
[25] Whistleblower Retaliation Checklist © Jacqueline Garrick

Gaslight (Figure 5) in which the heroine is manipulated into questioning her own perceptions of reality by her abusive husband. This tactic is also associated with bullies, sociopaths, narcissists, and emotional abusers who want to deflect their own wrongdoing and belittle or degrade the intelligence of their victims.[26] We have a natural sense to question and judge ourselves, which makes this technique particularly damaging because it gets the employee to start doubting themselves and questioning their own memories and beliefs. Be prepared to have your "opinion" or memory of events questioned by senior leaders or official investigators, no matter how friendly or charming they may seem!

Case Example: Jane had worked successfully for her organization for 10 years when along came Nancy who was very popular in the company and had influence with Jane's boss, Sally. Nancy asked Jane to move funds to from one contract to another. But, Jane saw that it would benefit Nancy's family. Jane thought this was a conflict of interest and that it would look like favoritism to other entities, so she refused and reported the concerns to the organization's compliance office to investigate. When Jane met with the investigator, he was very nice, but he made Jane feel as if she didn't know what she was talking about. She felt that the intimidation she reported was minimized. His interrogation was nerve-wracking for Jane who felt like she had to defend her credibility against Nancy's. When Sally found out about the complaint, things got worse for Jane. Sally told Jane that she was making too big a deal out of it and that Nancy was her friend, so she should drop her complaints and not risk the relationship. Sally also told Jane that it would not be good for the organization and she advised her to focus on her own career goals. Jane began to think she had made a mistake in saying anything about the funds to anyone.

Tip: Keeping notes and sending confirmation emails or memos about conversations can help you develop a record of the wrongdoing in real time. Anything date stamped becomes harder to dispute or minimize. This record will also help you document and explain why

---

[26] Stout, M. (2005) The Sociopath Next Door. Broadway Books. New York. P.94-97

your recall is so good and makes it harder to refute your memory of events. Your own notes and diaries can be used as contemporaneous evidence in most proceedings.

Mobbing – This happens when managers encourage or directly ask other employees (sometimes a subordinate) to monitor and report on the activities of the whistleblower or invade their private information (personnel folders or medical records). Creating a "mob mentality" incentivizes others to "gang up on" the whistleblower to gain or maintain favor with management. It can be done by copying

superiors, other managers, and non-essential peers on sensitive emails or other social media in attempts to intimidate, shame, or discredit the whistleblower. Studies show that this is a common feature of workplace bullying that involves spreading rumors, humiliation in front of others, and dismissiveness of the employee who blew the whistle.[27] The

Figure 6: Flying Monkey

term "flying monkeys"[28] has also been used to describe the behavior of subordinates who do the bidding of the more senior abusive manager. This behavior leads to more "group think" that heightens the sense of self-preservation of an expanding pool of co-workers who can be pressed into being co-conspirators or hostile to the whistleblower without knowing all the facts of the case. Carol Czarkowski, [29] a whistleblower, whose case goes back decades, still describes the mobbing and other toxic tactics of retaliation used against her as being "professionally gang raped."

---

[27] Workplace Bullying Institute. http://www.workplacebullying.org/. Accessed: January 21, 2018.

[28] From the 1939 Movie, The Wizard of Oz. The term has been adapted to denote the manipulated victims of narcissists. (Flying monkeys were the movie creatures that did the bidding of the "Wicked Witch of the West.") See Figure 6
http://freedomfromnarcissisticandemotionalabuse.weebly.com/blog/flying-monkeys. Accessed: January 21, 2018.

[29] Former Supervisory Contracting Officer and Whistleblower, Department of the Navy, Federal Circuit Decision with Precedence 03-3300

A common ruse of mobbing is to make it appear "fair and objective"[30] by convening a review board. But, then, members are hand-picked by the management team with an intended negative outcome for the whistleblower. The deck is stacked against you without the appearance of illegality. Other employees who participate or witness the wrongdoing and the subsequent retaliation become silent bystanders because they are fearful of being targeted themselves (a phenomenon related to the conspiracy of silence theory.) These employees may also begin to develop symptoms of anxiety and depression related to the survivor guilt that they feel when they know that they have been complicit in the harm being done to other and they did nothing to prevent it.

Another aspect of mobbing relates to when managers and/or co-workers inappropriately access an employee's private medical or benefits information and uses that information against the whistleblower. Although, this behavior is a violation of the Health Insurance Portability and accountability Act (HIPPA) it is nevertheless all too common as illustrated by the thousands of veterans/VA employees who have had their medical records illegally accessed by other VA employees, especially during an Administrative Investigation Board (AIB).[31] [32] The term "weaponized diagnosis"[33] has been used to describe what happens during investigations and in court cases when personnel folder information or a medical provider's notes are introduced to argue

---

[30]Under OPM rules that guide the Merit System Principles, it requires that an evaluation panel be fair and objective when selecting members to sit on the panel that reviews potential hiring actions.

[31] Volpe, M. VA regional manager accessed file that included whistle-blower's medical records. *The Daily Caller.* October 12. 2017. http://dailycaller.com/2017/10/12/va-regional-manager-accessed-file-that-included-whistle-blowers-medical-records/. Accessed: January 26, 2018.

[32] Waldman, A., Ornstein, C. Privacy violations rising at VA medical center. *National Public Radio. December 30, 2015.* https://www.npr.org/sections/health-shots/2015/12/30/461400692/patient-privacy-isn-t-safeguarded-at-veterans-medical-facilities. Accessed: January 26, 2018.

[33] Caplan, P., J. When Johnny and Jane Come Marching Home Blog. https://whenjohnnyandjanecomemarching.weebly.com/blog/psychiatrists-major-lobby-group-does-not-care-about-weaponized-diagnosis. November 11, 2012. Accessed: January 26, 2018.

that an employee is unfit or to informally humiliate them by gossiping about their medical condition(s) in the office.

Case Example: Millie was brought into a stymied organization to bring about cultural changes and innovation. Millie found several program deficiencies and wanted to make changes and hold employees more accountable for their goals. However, she was met with a great deal of resistance from the "old guard" who liked the way things had been done before Millie – who they considered an outsider – had arrived. She was identifying deficits with their programs and their performance, but because they had tenure, they also had influence and were able to use it to persuade senior leaders who had originally wanted change that they did not like having their deficiencies exposed. Leaders teamed up with other employees aligned with their views about Millie and asked them to bring complaints about her forward. Subordinates she was trying to hold accountable were asked to report back on Millie's travel expenses and time and attendance, and other coworkers began forwarding emails from Millie to her supervisor behind her back or copying them on replies. Co-workers left nasty notes disparaging her racial and ethnic background in the office. Millie was eventually moved to another assignment before leaving the agency when she found out that her family information was being involved. The program Millie was trying to change reverted back to its previous performance standards.

Tip: Do not feed into mobbing. Stay professional and courteous to your co-workers. Develop your own support network outside of the managements' sphere of influence, but do not expect others to stick their necks out for you. Remember that they also may be afraid of hostile and retaliatory leaders and everyone has their own comfort level, so do not be judgmental or burn any bridges. There may be others experiencing the same retaliation as you and teaming up with them could help, but this could take time. Form your own alliances carefully and selectively! Know who to trust! If you believe your HIPAA or other Privacy, Security or Breach Notifications Rules have been violated, you should report this to the HHS Office for Civil Rights. (See Appendix E.)

Marginalizing – Managers trying to discredit or silence a whistleblower will move them to more meager space (i.e. from an office to a cubical, no window/ventilation or temperature control) or detail them to a lesser, more menial assignment, or a more remote area. They may also be placed on Administrative Leave for prolonged periods of time further isolating them from professional support. Dr. Dale Klein in his book about retaliation at the VA, described his own isolation at work, "To sit in a room and stare at the walls. Every day. I had gone 16 continuous months without seeing a patient…The isolation was oppressive and almost unbearable."[34] He compares this mistreatment to the solitary confinement prisoners of war experience as emotionally traumatic. Another whistleblower compared it to being hijacked.

Other forms of marginalization are more situational. Managers will be dismissive of their work products or ideas as inferior in front of others (eye-rolling, watch-checking, talking over them), minimize their contributions, and not include them in important meetings or decisions that impact their area of responsibility. The whistleblower may be removed from having contact with patients (in a medical setting), customers (in a business), or other high-visibility positions (in government). Whistleblower correspondences will be trivialized.

Marginalization in the workforce has often been associated with acts of discrimination based on age, disability, race, ethnicity, religion, gender/LGBTQ or marital/family status. Under the law,[35] these employees are protected classes from discrimination and such instances constitute harassment that should be reported to EEO/EEOC. Whistleblowers have become a new class to be discriminated against because of their disclosures of wrongdoing and are protected from Prohibited Personnel Practices.

Case Example: Kris was a disabled African American female veteran who returned from her military deployment to her previous

---

[34] Klein, D.J. (2018) Scandals: Unmasking the Underbelly of the VA. Middletown, DE.
[35] Laws may vary from state to state and by jurisdiction regarding employment discrimination and court rulings. The EEOC follows and interprets employment discrimination based on Title VII of the Civil Rights Act of 1964.

job. After a few months home, however, Kris, suffered an on the job injury. Her organization was frustrated with her and her co-workers were resentful that they had already picked up her slack while she deployed. Now, they felt she was just being lazy and wanted special treatment. Managers felt that they had complied with the law and held her job while she was gone for her military service but asking for a "reasonable accommodation" was too much. The organization did not feel as if they had to offer her any more special treatment, so instead of returning her to her job with an accommodation, they moved her to another location where she had less authority and a smaller office. Kris filed an EEO complaint.

Tip: Document these changes in your own diary by noting the dates, times and locations of moves or changes to your job description. Take pictures of changed office space. Send courteous emails asking about missed meeting and blind copy yourself. Save those emails. Report violations to EEO/EEOC.

Shunning – Where marginalization physically isolates the whistleblower, shunning does it on an interpersonal and emotional level. It involves isolating and ostracizing whistleblowers from the team by not including them on correspondences, meeting invitations, or other activities is a manager's way of building walls between coworkers. Managers will ignore or dismiss emails or other communications from the whistleblower. It sends a message to the rest of the team that this person is "not important" or "tainted" and to stay away from them. When other staff have been solicited to mob an employee, or see them being marginalized, then fears of being associated with that person grows. Whistleblowers report being labeled as troublemakers, complainers, disgruntled, disruptive, disloyal, tainted or otherwise painted in a bad light to ruin their reputation among their peers and other managers.

Even though IG complaints are supposed to remain confidential, once an investigation begins, so does the rumor mill. No one wants to work with the person who is embroiled with a management disagreement. Thus, the whistleblowers social support further diminishes as they are not included in lunches or other social gatherings, conversations, or activities. Shunning also leads to breakdowns in trust between employees and disintegrates unit cohesion.

Case Example: Amanda had been at her organization for almost 20 years and was an effective program manager. She was well admired and respected until a new executive, Ben, came in as her supervisor. He immediately wanted more control over the resources Amanda managed. It was clear that his intentions were to shift funds to his own areas of interest and get his friends jobs. Several of Amanda's colleagues also were concerned and filed complaints. Amanda was immediately singled out by Ben as the whistleblower, although she was not actually the person who made the complaint. He would berate her in front of others, including junior staff and disparage her to senior leaders. He marginalized her by restricting her ability to attend meetings that she once led and took away her scope of responsibilities. Amanda sat in her office and felt isolated from the team and the mission she once cared about. Ben had painted her as a disgruntled troublemaker, so her colleagues (and friends) avoided her and fewer came to her office for fear of being seen, even if it were just to have lunch. It was not until an investigation concluded, two years later, that Ben was fired. But, due to the stress she suffered, Amanda resigned because she was unable to recover from the hostile work environment and filed a complaint with OSC.

Tip: Find other supportive social systems outside of your immediate work area. There are professional, civic/community, and religious organizations that offer opportunities to engage and who need your expertise and time. Find some other outlet for your positive energy and volunteer or join in. There might be an EAP available at work, but make sure you can count on confidentiality before you give details about your boss. A WoAP mentor can assist with supporting your resilience and finding you other resources.

Be self-aware. How are you handling conflict or any feedback from your supervisor? You should maintain an appropriate disposition and manage your expectations of your co-workers. Know your own shortfalls and blind spots as well as your leadership skills. A good source for self-actualization is the Gallup Clifton Strengths™ assessment tool[36] but there are other tools you may want to try too. This will help you see yourself (strengths and weaknesses) and how you interact with others.

Shunning is often the most harmful psychological impact that leads to distress, anxiety, depression, substance abuse, or suicidal thoughts. A mental health consultation might be warranted to handle this level of emotional turmoil. Treatment does work!

Devaluing – Manipulative managers will reduce a whistleblower's performance evaluation from previous higher levels and produce counseling statements based on bogus charges that were fabricated using mobbing tactics and counter-accusations. When managers lessen an employee's work assignments or have given them marginal tasks to complete that are not in line with the employee's job description, then managers feel justified in rating previously high performing employees lower because they are not excelling at their job descriptions. A lower performance evaluation also reduces opportunities for performance-based bonuses, training opportunities, promotions, or the ability to compete for other jobs. Accomplishments go unrecognized or credit is given to someone else. Plagiarism is tolerated. The whistleblower is held to a work standard that is not being fairly applied across equal ranks.

The ultimate goal of devaluation is to get rid of the whistleblower. Organizations can place the whistleblower on administrative leave, terminate an employee, or force someone to retire or resign. These drastic actions to devalue can also result in an employee being blackballed from their profession because future hiring managers will question the exiting circumstances of previous employment.

Termination – There are two primary standards for termination. In organizations that do not need to justify firing an employee, it can be done "at will." In other cases, there must be documented cause before an employee can be fired. Terminated employees in the private sector can sue for "wrongful termination" through the courts.

---

[36] https://www.gallupstrengthscenter.com/

Federal employees have different avenues for address than private sector employees and must go through OSC and MSPB. Depending upon the hiring authority or status that federal employees are under (i.e.: temporary, permanent, probationary, political, career, etc.) determines the level of protection from termination that they are afforded. However, civil servants are not without their termination risks regardless because management efforts can be manipulatively framed as "re-organization" or given "down-sizing" pretexts. Federal employees should be aware of their appointment status, such as whether they are permanent or temporary employees because this can determine if they can challenge a termination or not.

Resignation – In other cases, the stress of retaliation becomes too overwhelming and whistleblowers resign (which is what toxic organizations want you to do.) This is known as "Constructive Dismissal.[37] This is an important point to consider before you resign because you cannot just quit and then claim these damages. You must have some level of evidence that the working environment was so unusually adverse that a reasonable person would have felt compelled to resign, and that the organization either intended to force such a resignation or had actual knowledge of the intolerable persistent working conditions. A whistleblower claiming to have been constructively dismissed must document that the work environment that gave rise to the resignation was sufficiently extraordinary and egregious to overcome the normal motivation of a competent and reasonable person to remain on the job. Additionally, the resignation cannot be based on a single event, (i.e. one poor performance evaluation) but rather on a series of events and hostile conditions, unless there was a violent crime committed against the whistleblower. File a police report immediately.

In addressing whether an employer's conduct amounts to sufficiently intolerable or egregious working conditions to permit constructive

---

[37] Constructive Dismissal (termination or discharge) information is from: http://employment.findlaw.com/losing-a-job/constructive-dismissal-and-wrongful-termination.html. Accessed January 8, 2018.

dismissal, courts focus on several factors including:

- Whether the employee was requested or required to participate in illegal activity;
- Whether the employer duly acknowledged or investigated the employee's complaints;
- The nature of the employer's illegal conduct; and
- The passage of time between the allegedly illegal conduct and the employee's resignation.

Case Example: Leslie had been a doctor in several rural areas when she took a job in a larger hospital system. Leslie liked her patients and wanted to be able to help them feel better. She had not been at her new job all that long when she discovered that many of her patients were on multiple medications and opioids. When she raised her concerns with management about over-prescribing practices at the hospital to expedite visits, she was immediately told that she did not understand her job. Her previous performance evaluations had been stellar, but after she made her disclosure, she was given a poor performance evaluation and placed on a developmental plan for being disruptive. Leslie made several other attempts to address what she felt was over-medicating patients, but eventually felt that it was too career damaging and left her job. However, she used her documentation on improper pharmaceutical prescribing practices to file a case for constructive dismissal.

Tip: It is hard not to react to every little injustice or insult, but it is best to focus on the big picture items. Make sure you are not insubordinate or noncompliant with policies or regulations governing your organization. Document your objections to any poor or reduced performance evaluations or denied opportunities. File a grievance or ask for a higher-level review. Challenge any counter-accusations of impropriety made against you. Submit your rebuttal to the same authority that your manager submits your counseling statement. This is information that an attorney will need for defending your case and in asking for damages.

Double-binding – This one is tricky because it feels like it could be restorative, but make no mistake, it is setting you up for failure. Truly toxic leaders will give whistleblowers who have been blocked from previous assignments, new tasks to complete, but with inadequate resources or support. They will allow them to take on a new venture, but then will accuse them of failing or find some fault with what they did. At first, these tasks may seem like the organization values the employee because they trust them with a difficult task. But, these tasks are assigned knowing that the possibility for success is limited, thereby, giving management the opportunity to grade the whistleblower with poor performance marks (devaluing) or if successful to ignore those accomplishments as "going above and beyond." It is a no-win situation for the whistleblower.

Case Example: Tom was a hard worker by nature and was very committed to his mission. He was in the business of helping people and took that role and responsibility very seriously. When he felt that his office was using wasteful systems and had a lack of accountability, he made his disclosures to senior managers. They immediately removed him from his job, but he filed a whistleblower retaliation complaint and his agency was forced to reinstate him. Tom thought that his troubles were behind him. When he returned to work, he was given a new job to complete. However, this new mission had been experiencing multiple management problems, cost-overruns and was in jeopardy of being cancelled. At first, Tom thought the agency was showing that they had faith in him to fix their problems, but when his requests for resources were denied, he soon realized that he was being set up to fail. Miraculously, Tom achieved his goals and saved the program. But, he was not given the opportunity to continue with the program, which was turned over to a colleague to manage instead. Tom was detailed to another ambiguous assignment, which became his career pattern until he left the organization.

Tip: Do not suck it up. No matter how much you think that you can prove them wrong about you by being successful, it will not reinstate your career standing or stop the retaliation. You are already on management's radar screen as a whistleblower and they are on a path to protect themselves and the organization from the limelight you cast. Therefore, you need to document the problems with the assignment, offer solutions, but drive on as best as you can. Give status updates and continue to cite inefficiencies with the task. Do not be insubordinate or flat out refuse to complete an assigned task. Be prepared for your hard work to sit on a shelf.

Blackballing – Sometimes also called blacklisting, this is a Prohibited Personnel Practice under the law that involves obstructing a person's ability to compete for a position, but barring having a photograph of someone tossing your application in the trash, it is hard to prove. Furthermore, it can be difficult for the whistleblower to leave the office or the organization that perpetrated the wrongdoing since the whistleblower's reputation has already been harmed by previous devaluing tactics (especially related to administrative leave, termination, or resignation as previously noted). Cases will get slow-rolled and/or stonewalled to keep the whistleblower in limbo as patience, options, and resources run out.

If the disclosure has made its way into the public domain, then accounts of the whistleblower's credibility, character, and motivation have been scrutinized by media outlets or social networks. This damage to the whistleblower's professional reputation and personnel record makes hiring managers in other offices reluctant to want to hire the whistleblower. Organizations have been known to blackball whistleblowers to further impede their ability to compete for jobs in related industries or fields of expertise because they do not want the whistleblower to have access or influence in the same circles.

Case Example: By the time John was ready to leave his hostile work environment, he found it difficult to find another job in his profession. His reputation previously had been damaged by managers who labeled his as a complainer and disgruntled employee after he reported waste, fraud, and abuse. While investigations and mediations had taken years to complete, John had moved around his organization without ever getting new job descriptions or performance evaluations that reflected his actual work. Therefore, his official personnel folder was incongruent with his resume. It took John several years and a move to a different location to find satisfying employment again.

Tip: Overcoming this form of retaliation requires resilience because it can otherwise lead to a foreshortened sense of future, hopelessness and helplessness. Reinventing yourself can be a challenge, but it means either hanging in there for your case to come to fruition and being vindicated or moving on to another organization, career field, or location. Get a copy of your official personnel folder so that you know what it contains and ask for a list of who else has accessed your information. Keep copies of documents and emails related to your performance. Get witness statements from anyone who knows about the retaliation as soon as you can because witnesses will not recall events years later when cases come before a judge, or they might have moved away, retired, or died. Monitor your social media footprint. If you are aware of actual blackballing, document those instances because it can be considered by a judge if you are claiming damages with your case.

Accusing – This involves developing counter accusations of insubordination, misuse of funds, inaccurate travel expenses, or unauthorized use of vacation/sick leave (including FMLA[38]) to discredit the professionalism of the whistleblower or to justify causation for termination. This is sometimes also referred to as "keeping book." Previous attempts to devalue a whistleblower, may lead to counseling statements and performance improvement plans placed in their official personnel record. Many whistleblowers report that they have received official counseling for being "disruptive" because of their whistleblowing activities. They become the scapegoat of the wrongdoing that they reported, or any other organizational failure is blamed on them.

Counter accusations put the whistleblower on the defense and holds them to a higher standard of accountability than is being applied to other employees. Mobbing is used to develop these accusations by

---

[38] Family and Medical Leave Act

having employees "spy" on each other and find errors in accounting for expenses or time and attendance – even if they are minor errors or typos. These accusations can turn into legal actions and charges against the whistleblower based upon the nature of the information disclosed and how it was obtained. It can also involve charges related to inappropriately using office time or equipment for personal gain, including whistleblowing. So, do your whistleblowing on your own dime, especially if you are talking to the press or even Congress (unless you have been subpoenaed by Congress or directed through your agency to do so). Otherwise, these are not protected disclosures. This includes union activities.

These accusations can be life-altering because being involved in intensive legal processes is expensive and adjudication (and recovery) can take years. It can make the whistleblower a public figure; open to all kinds of scrutiny, especially on social media, and a target for violence. Some whistleblowers become subjects of the legal investigation themselves and have gone to jail for their initial complicity.

<u>Case Example:</u> Millie, who had previously experienced mobbing, soon found that those who were spying on her were using that information to justify bringing charges against her. Those claims were turned into counter-accusations of very minor infractions and an investigation into Millie's conduct soon ensued. Millie had to hire her own attorney to defend herself, her job, and her reputation. Although, there were a few people willing to stand up for her, no one in management defended her. She spent thousands of dollars of her own money and when her employer offered a settlement, she decided that she would never be able to work for them again without having to watch over her shoulder, so she resigned.

<u>Tip</u>: Refute these counter-accusations as accurately as possible with the documentation that you have kept. Take copious notes at meetings as this contemporaneous evidence is considered valuable because of its real-time accounting. Be careful not to engage in certain activities while on the clock if it is precluded by organizational policy, such as promoting a union or talking to the

media. Work on your case on your own time and do not spend organizational funds unless authorized, such as if OIG asks you to assist or Congress subpoenas you. If you have made any accounting or time-keeping errors, correct them immediately. See if professional insurance will cover you. If so, buy it. You should consult with a private attorney if legal actions are being taken against you.

Physical and Emotional Violence
– On average, 2 million employees report experiencing workplace violence each year as characterized by "any act or threat of physical violence, harassment, intimidation, or other threatening disruptive behavior that occurs at the work site."[39] Whistleblowers have had property damaged (i.e. cars keyed), derogatory and nasty notes left on their desks, been stalked, or had family members harassed, including their children. They have been subjected to intimidation and

Figure 7: DC Metro train, 2017

manipulation by people with influence. They have been yelled at, defamed, and disparaged in open settings or privately bullied. They have had their confidentiality or privacy violated so that the information could be used to humiliate and discredit them. Sexual harassment and assaults have occurred, especially in closed environments when abuses of power and manipulation go unchecked, such as previously noted with MST.

Noteworthy, there is a legal standard and definition for harassment, but not bullying. Bullying is not illegal, although unethical. It is a harmful interpersonal hostility that is intentional and occurs frequently and persistently. Bullying is a component of a hostile work environment, organizational dysfunction, critical and ill-

---

[39] OSHA. Workplace Violence. https://www.osha.gov/SLTC/workplaceviolence/ Accessed: March 18, 2018

equipped management and insufficient personnel training that allows for spying, plagiarism, favoritism, and scapegoating in the workplace. In and of itself, however, bullying does not cross a threshold for illegality and must be addressed through different channels (i.e.: human resources or the union) than harassment, which can be reported to law enforcement.[40]

When the stakes are high, alleged reports of whistleblowers being murdered have surfaced, such as the famous case of Karen Silkwood whose car mysteriously crashed in 1974, when she was on her way to meet a reporter. In 2016, of the over 5,000 workplace deaths, 792 were the result of intentional harm, 500 were homicides and 291 were suicides, which all have been on the rise since 2011.[41] Whistleblowers have left suicide notes identifying retaliation and its impacts as the cause of their deaths, such as with Dr. Chris Kirkpatrick who was fired from the Tomah VA Medical Center after reporting on the over-medicating of patients. He died by suicide in 2009 while embattled with VA. (See section on *Warning Signs of Harm to Self and Others*.)

Figure 8: Artwork by Rachel Garrick

If the case becomes very public, the harassment or cyber bullying can become more widespread - involving strangers, news pundits, or cloaked co-workers on

[40] Workplace Bullying Institute.
http://www.workplacebullying.org/wbiresearch/wbistudies/#tactics. Accessed January 6, 2018.
[41] Bureau of Labor Statistics. Table 2. Fatal occupational injuries for selected events or exposures, 2011-16. https://www.bls.gov/news.release/cfoi.t02.htm. Accessed: March 18,2018.

social media. This will require a thick skin and outlets for coping, like painting in Figure 8.

Case Example: Maria's boss was a known bully, but management saw him as effective, so his bad behavior continued. He treated Maria and her team with disrespect and would yell and scream at them. He would send subordinates on personal errands and used official funds for personal matters. Maria was one of the youngest members of the team and one of only a few females. One day, her boss was being particularly aggressive with Maria in front of other employees. He was embarrassing her, and she began to cry. At the encouragement of others, she reported his harassment and his other abusive habits. Once an investigation ensued, Maria's boss focused on her as the complainant and treated her with even greater disrespect. When Maria discussed her situation with a new female executive that had come onboard, her abusive boss was immediately moved to another location until the investigation concluded, which found enough evidence of bullying and harassment to remove him from work.

Tip: Report any threats, damages to property, or assaults to local law enforcement *immediately!* Cyber-bullying should be reported to the FBI. Get witness statements. If you need an Order of Protection get one from your local jurisdiction (rules will vary by state). Do NOT waiver on this! If you can document harassing phone calls or stalking, for example, consider sending a Cease and Desist Letter that warns the perpetrator that their behavior is unwanted and infringes on your rights. (Templates are online or contact a law firm.) This documents the harassing behavior and puts the agency and perpetrator(s) on notice. You must have evidence, otherwise you risk a "he said/she said" quandary.

Surviving these toxic tactics requires that whistleblowers have a good strategic plan for their disclosures along with a strong commitment to the justice that they seek for themselves or the greater good and a well-developed sense of personal resilience and social support. Keep in mind that this is a long-haul process that can takes years to resolve. Look for ways to settle!

Resilience Risk Impacts of Retaliation

As whistleblowers experience the various forms of *Toxic Tactics* to get them to drop their complaints or leave the organization while they continue to press for justice, there is a toll that this commitment takes on their lives and their psyche. WoA categorizes these risk impacts to your resilience as outlined in Table 1.

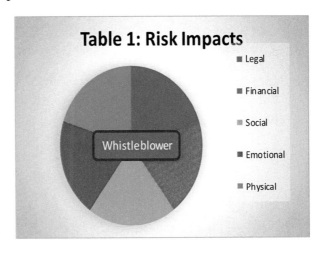

Table 1: Risk Impacts

Whistleblower

- Legal
- Financial
- Social
- Emotional
- Physical

You must balance these risks!

Legal – First and foremost, employees need to see whistleblowing as a legal process and know the laws related to the wrongdoing identified and applicable protections for whistleblowers. Unfortunately, whistleblowing does not usually start out that way. It usually starts out naively. An employee sees a problem and wants to fix it. There are warning signs all around us to "See something, say something" (Figure 3) and organizations provide ethics training that encourages the reporting of wrongdoing and have offices dedicated to these investigations.

But, as soon as you realize that the wrongdoing is a bigger problem with greater repercussions than you thought, start thinking and acting legally. Protect yourself and your family from reprisal. Know the applicable federal, state, or local laws, rules and ethics of your organization or profession. Know what evidence is needed, how to legally obtain it, and to whom to report the wrongdoing. Be prepared to monitor for *Toxic Tactics* related to counter accusations, marginalization, and devaluing of your performance and address those issues as they arise. Protect yourself emotionally from gaslighting, shunning and mobbing, which can be disheartening and/or demoralizing. These tactics can have an emotional impact and become a source of damages for "pain and suffering" in your settlement, so document it. Unlike other remuneration at settlement, anything for "physical sickness that caused the emotional distress" is non-taxable[42] so be prepared to prove it.

❖ **Note - Hiring an Attorney**
If you decide you need to hire an attorney to represent you in an administrative process, you should consider several factors:

- Experience and expertise of the attorney or the law firm. Is your case in their scope of work and where can they represent you? For example, some attorneys cannot bring cases to Federal Court or do not have Security Clearances to handle secret information.
- Be prepared to identify your desired outcome (Cease and Desist Letter, Order of Protection, OSC/MSPB/EEOC representation)? This will help the attorney manage your expectations for damages and inform you about the options available to you.
- Get recommendations from other whistleblowers for legal representation. Who did they hire and why? How satisfied were they with the performance of the attorney and the outcome? Check out the law firm's website and look for any reviews. What has been the firms track record in cases like yours? Contact the ABA for a referral.
- What are the fees? Is there a consultation fee or is the first visit free? Is there a retainer fee and the need for you to sign an agreement? Are you ready to do that?
- Do you have insurance that will cover legal fees? If not, how will you raise the money?

---

[42] IRS Publication 4345. https://www.irs.gov/pub/irs-pdf/p4345.pdf. Accessed: March 11, 2018.

- Most firms cannot and do not work on contingencies no matter the percentage recovered you offer them. Be prepared to spend $100,000 for a case that goes to MSPB/Court.
- Consider at least three firms before hiring one. Depending on the complexity of your case, you may need to consider multiple firms.
- Research the laws you feel were violated and know what protections you have when making disclosures. The more organized you are, the less time the attorney needs to spend developing your case. Have your narrative of events, all supporting evidence of wrongdoing and damages, and a timeline ready.
- If you cannot afford to hire an attorney, do you have the time and ability to represent yourself, *pro se*[43]? Does the administrative or judicial process you will need to engage allow for pro se representation? Do you know the laws and rules? Can you present just the facts? Is it too emotional?
- Does your family support you? Do they understand the implications of a long drawn out legal battle? What sacrifices might they have to make?

Financial – Since legal cases can take years to resolve (while retaliation persists), there may be a financial impact to whistleblowing, especially when legal representation can cost upwards of $100,000, if you cannot represent yourself. Whistleblowers find that they are suddenly not selected for training opportunities or advancements, performance appraisals are diminished, and bonuses are nixed or minimal. Those impacts need to be calculated as well because they have financial implications related to your lifetime earnings potential. Whistleblowers who are

---

[43] Pro se means that you are representing yourself in a legal situation without an attorney. This is permissible in most courts or with the OSC/MSPB process, but not necessarily advisable. This will depend on your own relevant knowledge, legal experience, and time to devote to your case.

terminated and then blackballed, may find it hard to get other jobs. This blackballing further impacts family functioning, such as a spouse's need for employment, health insurance coverage, rent or mortgage payments, vacations, child care, college funds, retirement plans, caregiving, or other family obligations. The family whistleblowing breadwinner may begin to feel burdensome and a liability to their own family's security and may take financial risks, such as in selecting poor performing investments or gambling. Vulnerable families have fallen victim to credit card, lending, and other frauds and scams that upsell and over-promise results, like timeshares or student loans.

Social – Shunning often leaves the whistleblower isolated in the workplace and diminishes their sense of belongingness, purpose, and meaning. This ostracism can leak into other professional spectrums as coworkers do not want to be tainted by being associated with a legal battle or media frenzy. Feelings of humiliation and embarrassment resulting from the *Toxic Tactics*, lead to whistleblowers who avoid social situations and activities that remind them of the lost professional status that they once enjoyed. This isolation not only occurs at work, but at home with family or in the community, such as avoiding going to church or playing golf. This further alienates and isolates a whistleblower from their normal support system. Additionally, it can devastate family members who did not anticipate the financial and social status losses from reporting wrongdoing. Divorce and estrangement from family members or lost friendships have been reported in some instances of whistleblowing.

Emotional – Retaliation is a traumatic experience. The stress and strain of a legal battle and the impacts it has on the financial and social status of the whistleblower can lead to emotional distress and psychological disorders. Feeling burdensome on others, loss of meaning, purpose, or hope; extreme stress because of retaliation or a hostile environment; ostracism at work, home and community; anger and frustration over injustices; guilt over not being able to protect others from harm; and the loss of identity that comes with whistleblowing takes a psychological toll. Dealing with the effects of gaslighting, marginalization, devaluing and double-binding can lead to nightmares or intrusive thoughts about perpetrators or the harm being done to public safety, individual welfare, or financial fraud costs. Counter-accusing and threats of violence results in "paranoia" about risks to safety for oneself and loved ones and can leave employees hyper-vigilant, alert, and/or sleepless. Studies show that whistleblowers can suffer from depression, anxiety, insomnia, posttraumatic stress disorder (PTSD), substance abuse, and suicidal ideation.[44] These impacts can erode resilience and cause further emotional decline.

The resultant losses of whistleblowing in terms of career status, professional identity and personal roles, and ability to be self-efficacious require a grieving process similar to the death of a loved one. Whistleblowing has been called "career suicide."[45] There has been a death in your life, just not a physical one. Life after whistleblowing will never be the same and is a major adjustment. Overcoming the stigma associated with whistleblower retaliation and breaking down the barriers to seeking-help can be added challenges to finding the right support and treatment. It will take time and assistance to persevere and regain a sense of purpose and a commitment to justice. Surviving and finding a new normal can be achieved with a WoAP mentor. It may also require a mental health professional to diagnose and treat any arising psychological conditions related to your retaliation stressors. When selecting a clinician, make sure that they understand the dynamics of whistleblower retaliation and recognize it as a traumatic stressor. Medication may help with sleep disorders, depression, PTSD, or anxiety. Suicidal ideation or behaviors should always be addressed urgently with professional care.

If whistleblowing has caused a crisis of faith, then talking to a member of the clergy should also be considered. Loss of hope, meaning, or purpose for some people is tied to their sense of spirituality and is a component of emotional well-being. If religion

---

[44] Garrick, J. *Peer support for whistleblowers.* Federal Practitioner. July 2017 Vol. 34, No. 7. 38-41

[45] Soeken K, Soeken D. *A survey of whistleblowers: their stressors and coping strategies.* Laurel, Maryland: Association of Mental Health Specialties; 1987.

has been a source of comfort, do not discount it now. Rituals that honor memory or commemorate a loss can be helpful. Finding new ways to maintain those rites or adding new ones can be restorative and foster resilience. Using prayer, yoga, meditation, or mindfulness techniques can help emotionally regulate your stress level, add to your sense of homeostasis, give you time to self-actualize, and feel in charge of your life and your destiny.

Physical – It is no secret that emotional stress can lead to physical health ailments as well. The brain chemistry changes related to experiencing trauma are well documented among other types of survivors and can be associated with whistleblowing as well. This physical change in brain chemistry, (i.e. release of adrenalin) if prolonged, can become internally toxic to our bodies.[46] As mentioned, whistleblower investigations and legal battles can take years and involve prolonged exposure to a hostile work environment, which can have an impact on our health as similarly documented in war veterans and first responders. Whistleblowers have reported subsequent diagnosis such as migraines, muscle tension, arthritis, fibromyalgia, chronic fatigue syndrome, gastrointestinal conditions, increased blood pressure and cardiovascular disease.[47] These conditions should be taken seriously as well and treated by a qualified physician. A dentist should also be consulted for symptoms of teeth grinding or TMJ.[48] Multiple studies have found that there is correlation between severe mental disorders, such as depression and PTSD to increases in morbidity and mortality among those patients.[49]

As whistleblowers develop their *Whistleblower Strategic Plan* (Appendix C), mitigating these potential risk impacts should be considered and monitored. If a whistleblower case moves through

---

[46] Schnurr, P.P., Green, B.L. (2004) Trauma and Health: Physical Health Consequences of Exposure to Extreme Stress. American Psychological Association. Washington, DC.
[47] Garrick, J. *Peer support for whistleblowers.* Federal Practitioner. July 2017 Vol.34, No. 7. 38-41
[48] Temporomandiblar Joint Syndrome (TMJ) – pain and inflammation of the jaw, sometimes associated with stress.
[49] World Health Organization. (2015) Meeting Report on Excess Mortality in Persons with Severe Mental Disorders. Fountain House. Geneva, Switzerland.

the MSPB (for government) or the civilian courts, there are potential awards for damages in an effort "to make a whistleblower whole." So, it is important to track any medical or other expenses related to your retaliation recovery costs.

Warning Signs of Harm to Self and/or Others

In rare and extreme cases, when the risk impacts have overwhelmed whistleblowers, especially when wrongdoing prevails and retaliation wins, whistleblowers have inappropriately and violently struck back. In such cases, employees have engaged in espionage, sabotage, violence in the workplace, or have died by suicide at the work site. These adverse events can occur when management does not take its organizational climate seriously and is not prepared to handle disclosures of wrongdoing properly. <u>Immediate intervention is required, and threats of harm should be reported to law enforcement.</u>

Suicide Prevention

According to the Centers for Disease Control and Prevention (CDC), Suicide is the 10th leading cause of death in America, and averages 13.4 per 100,000 people or just over 42,700 Americans a year.[50] The rates increase among younger, white, males, and then among an aging population, so think of suicide age ranges as occurring along an inverted Bell Curve. Men are more likely to die by suicide because they usually chose a more lethal means (guns),

IS PATH WARM?
I - Ideation
S - Substance Abuse
P - Purposelessness
A - Anxiety
T - Trapped
H - Hopelessness
W - Withdrawal
A - Anger
R - Recklessness
M - Mood Changes

---

[50] CDC. Suicide: Facts at a Glance. (2015) https://www.cdc.gov/violenceprevention/pdf/suicide-datasheet-a.pdf. Accessed: January 22, 2018.

while women are more likely to attempt suicide with pills. However, according to VA 2017 data, female veterans have a much greater rate of suicide than their civilian counterparts. In general, veterans and military personnel have a higher suicide rate than non-veterans, which may be attributable to their familiarity with weapons. There have been numerous news reports of veterans who have died by suicide at a VA facility when they felt denied proper care or benefits. Less information has been reported as to the number of civilian employees who have died by suicide at work or because of workplace hostilities, retaliation, and/or discrimination. Regardless, there are risk factors related to suicide that WoAP mentors should be aware of and able to monitor. The following insights into those risk factors are based on the American Association of Suicidology (AAS)[51] and other materials published on their website. The AAS offers the mnemonic "IS PATH WARM?" to help remember the warning signs of suicide.

Suicide Risk Factors:

- A history of mental health problems or suicide attempts for that person or within their family

- A history of substance abuse or an increased use of substances

- Risk taking behavior – driving too fast, unsafe sex. *For whistleblowers, WoA includes workaholic behavior*

- Depression, grief, loss of hope, no sense of future, shame, and feeling like a failure or trapped in a no-win situation (investigations can feel endless and overwhelming)

- Anxiety (ruminating and excessive worry, nightmares) or extreme stress

- Unresolved trauma (PTSD) or anger

---

[51] AAS. http://www.suicidology.org/. Accessed January 7, 2018.

- Helplessness, worthlessness, and feeling like a burden on friends and/or family

- Relationship problems at home (infidelity, divorce, domestic violence) or at work (termination, retaliation, discrimination, harassment, bullying, or abuse)

- Financial and/or legal problems

- Physical illness or complaints or pain, including changes in appetite and sleep

- Access to lethal means (law enforcement or military personnel/veterans and firearms or medical staff and drugs – legal or illicit)

Warning Signs of Suicide:

- Talking/writing/posting/texting about any of the risk factors and wanting to hurt/kill oneself and how people would be better off without them. (Social media is a good monitoring tool. Look for what might sound like a suicide note.)

- Planning for suicide (when and where)

- Obtaining lethal means (buying a gun, stockpiling pills or poisons, rope)

- Withdrawing from family, friends, coworkers, and professional or civic activities

- Giving away treasured possessions or pets

- Updating wills, investments, and insurance policies (sometimes multiple times)

- Loss of pleasures (anhedonia) in activities, hobbies, social events or sex.

- Isolating from others (shunning, marginalizing, and humiliation are related to this.)

- Changes in mood or personality (sometimes happiness after depression can seem like someone is recovering, however, they should continue to be monitored because a suicide plan can be seen as a relief and uplifts the person who now feels empowered to die.)

Violence/Harm to Others

Like suicide, harm and violence towards others happen along a similar trajectory, although at a significantly lesser rate. However, harm in the workplace has been known to occur in several formats, such as espionage or sabotage, but physical violence has been a growing trend as well as. Whistleblowers may report feeling violent because of retaliation or experience violence by co-workers who want to intimidate or humiliate the whistleblower. Emotions can run extremely high when wrongdoing cover ups are exposed, especially if there is a potential for criminal charges, incarceration, and fines.

Violence – What to Look For:

- History of violence (domestic/child, physical or verbal abuse or criminal activity)

- Psychosis (inability to recognize reality, paranoia, delusional) or personality disorders (antisocial)

- Anger, fits of rage, belligerent outbursts, insubordination, coworker hostility

- Severe depression and loss of hope, faith, or sense of justice in the world

- Unrealistic expectations, frustrations, and blames others or self (suicidal)

- Obsessive negative thinking (stalking, harassing with calls or messages) especially in thoughts of seeking revenge or glory or making a "hit list" of transgressors

- Sending threatening messages to transgressors or vengeful social media posts about individuals or the organization, especially leaking private information

- Substance abuse and other high-risk behaviors (gambling), recklessness while driving, inappropriate sexual activity

- Apathetic about self-care (hygiene) or environment, no motivation (attendance, productivity, or performance problems emerge)

- Theft of organizational property/coworkers' belongings or disabling equipment.

- Interest in weapons and obtaining firearms, bringing weapons to the workplace

Take all threats of harm to self or others seriously and report them!

Call 911

Security Clearances are a reason many whistleblowers fear speaking out or seeking help. There is stigma associated with admitting to mental health issues and it can be hard to overcome this barrier. Employees should know that less than 1% of the population with a security clearance has ever lost it because of a mental health diagnosis when answering Standard Form 86, Question 21.

DoD advises to:
Respond "No" if the psychological counseling was strictly related to:
- Grief, marital or family concerns
- Adjustments from service in a combat zone
- Being a victim of sexual assault

Respond "Yes" for any other counseling for an emotional or psychological health concern taking place in the past seven years, along with additional information related to care or treatment received.

For more DoD information see:
http://www.realwarriors.net/active/treatment/clearance.php

Figure 9: Advertisement, Arlington National Cemetery Metro Station, Virginia, 2018

If they try to take your clearance away as reprisal under the pretext of "psychological conditions" get a complete psychological exam by an independent, credentialed clinician.

Resilience in Overcoming the Whistleblower Risk Impacts

In the *Risk Impacts of Retaliation* section of this guide, WoA explains what those risks look like and how things may play out with "You" in the center balancing it all. The good news is that resilience can be built, maintained, and sustained across all of those domains as well.

What is resilience?

Some experts have categorized it as the "bounce back" after adversity, but at WoA, we believe for any skill to have "bounce" it needs to first be inflated. Think of a ball with not enough air, when you try to bounce it, it rolls or goes off in wrong direction, but with the right amount of air, it scores!

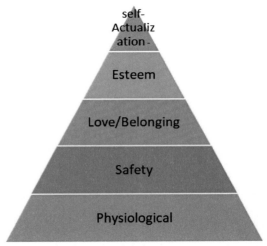

Figure 10: Maslow's Hierarchy of Needs

Resilience is the state of mind, body, and spirit that allows a person to overcome adversity and experience posttraumatic growth.

Resilience can be built, maintained, and sustained to face adversity and be rejuvenated in its post traumatic growth. However, there are important skills for building resilience that a whistleblower and their WoAP mentor should consider as outlined in Figure 10 demonstrating Abraham Maslow's Hierarchy of Needs.[52] According to Maslow, for humans to be healthy, we need to have our physiological needs met, feel safe, know we are loved, have self-esteem, and become self-actualized. As noted, whistleblowers face many challenges to their resilience through *Toxic Tactics* employed

---

[52] Maslow, A.H. (1954) Motivation and Personality. Harper. New York.

by managers or organizations. As with facing any of life's hardships, overcoming the pain of losing one's role or identity or surviving a hostile environment, whistleblowers can use their resilience skills across the same domains that are at risk from the impacts of retaliation.

Resilience Skills:

Legal – A key component of resilience is your self-actualization, which is about being aware of your moral compass and your sense of ethics. As a whistleblower, you already should be proud of how you have acted and the moral courage you have demonstrated. (Maslow is!) You have been altruistic in identifying harm to others or the public. You have followed the laws, rules, regulations, and ethics of the United States, your organization, and your own family or religious values. Your sense of right and wrong drove you to act when others did not. Those are admirable qualities that will serve you well throughout this process. Stay true to the ideals that got you started and they will see you through.

Financial – Our financial stability drives our sense of safety. At the base of the Maslow pyramid, is our physiological needs for food, shelter, and clothing. Being able to satisfy those needs makes us feel safe. It allows us to build relationships and our self-esteem as we further developed our sense of self-actualization. Although, whistleblowing can threaten our financial security, our sense of financial mental health can be preserved by the steps we take to ensure our financial future. This can be accomplished through appropriate financial planning with a certified advisor, which can be empowering and help to determine the steps that we can take in designing our *Whistleblower Strategic Plan*. Mapping out financial resources and needs can help visualize the decision-making process.

Social – Our sense of belonging, ability to contribute, and being respected and loved are crucial to our resilience. It is why peer support and the WoAP mentor are the cornerstones of WoA. You need to know who in your life supports you and can assist you in what could be a prolonged whistleblower process. Family, friends, co-workers, professional and/or civic associates, teachers, yoga instructors, chaplains, lawyers, doctors, social workers, financial planners, and your WoAP mentor might be part of your network. You should take time to think about who these people are in your life (or if they need to be) and how and when to be in contact with them and be mindful of their boundaries and beliefs. You must be willing to hear all feedback, even when you do not agree with it. Avoid being defensive with people who are trying to help you. Validate what you have heard and save it, even if you do disagree. It might not seem relevant at that time, but it may in the future. Do not burn bridges with people who do not see the wrongdoing as you do. They may have other guidance or insights to offer and might be more helpful in the future as more facts are brought to light. Remember that you are not the only one who might be suffering from the *Toxic Tactics*. If someone else's negativity is bringing you down, be honest about how it makes you feel and let them know what you need from them to help you cope. Be clear about your boundaries too. Know who you can call at 2AM when you can't sleep and who you should make an appointment to see for advice.

Emotional – Remaining optimistic will be an important factor in protecting your self-esteem. Relying on your sense of humor and ability to see irony will help heal the wounds of retaliation, discrimination, and injustice. Keeping a positive attitude will help you reframe situations, refute irrational beliefs, identify options and make clear decisions. Keep things in perspective and keep your faith. Identify the things that keep you motivated or make you happy. Stay engaged with them! The situation that you are in does not determine who you are regardless of the victimization associated with devaluing, shunning, and marginalizing tactics. Your process of becoming more self-actualized will grow from your individual ability to be innovative and creative with how you handle stress and preserve your dignity. You will feel empowered by your *Whistleblower Strategic Plan.*

Physical - You should not take your health for granted. While under the stress of retaliation, discrimination or a hostile work environment, you need to maintain your physiological needs and keep yourself safe. You should eat and drink right, do not smoke, rest, relax, and have fun. Do not neglect the people who are important to you or your favorite pastime. Try a new hobby. Get exercise or learn to meditate. This does not have to be expensive – a walk in the park is free. If you are experiencing any health ailments, consult your physician. Be vigilant, stress can affect your health and wellbeing in many ways. Also see a dentist, you might be grinding your teeth and not realize it.

Don't Bristle at the Whistle: A New Employee Engagement Paradigm for Organizations

"That makes me bristle" is what one senior corporate security officer said when asked about handling whistleblower cases. This reaction is indicative of the negative image and stereotypes of whistleblowers when they are shunned, labeled, and mischaracterized. Even Microsoft Windows Word ™ offers negative synonyms for whistleblower (See Figure 11.)

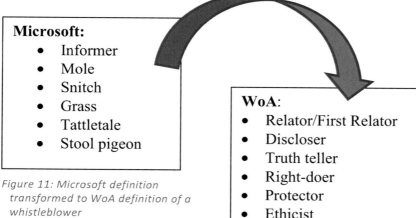

Microsoft:
- Informer
- Mole
- Snitch
- Grass
- Tattletale
- Stool pigeon

WoA:
- Relator/First Relator
- Discloser
- Truth teller
- Right-doer
- Protector
- Ethicist

Figure 11: Microsoft definition transformed to WoA definition of a whistleblower

However, based on WoA experience and whistleblower literature and laws, WoA advocates for changing those defining words to the more positive descriptors indicated in Figure 11.

A paradigm shift is needed when thinking and talking about whistleblowers. Under an Organization Development construct that values Change Management and Employee Engagement concepts,[53] a whistleblower program should be integrated into any Total Quality Management or Lean Six Sigma for continuous process improvement success. Human Resources, comptrollers and performance managers should be working together. Simply put, this could save time, money, and lives.

Heroes Too:

First Relators = First Responders

When WoA calls whistleblowers *the "First Relators" of wrongdoing,* it is meant to align them to First Responders (police, fire, and rescue) who risk their  own well-being for the common good. We think of First Responders as our community heroes who have saved lives and protected property. First Relators do similar thing, but in a different manner, yet end up facing some of the same risks to their own well-being.

WoA hopes to change the conversation about whistleblowing so that First Relators can receive the similar recognition and assistance as First Responders. The medical and legal communities need to see their traumas from retaliation, in the same way that they see the witnessing of harm or persecution in other populations as resulting in pain and suffering.

---

[53] See the Organization Development Network for more information on these concepts at http://www.odnetwork.org/page/WhatIsOD. Accessed January 22, 2018.

Part III – Peer Support

WoA Peer (WoAP) Support

Survivors with a common or shared experience relate to each other in a way that others do not. Previous studies on peer-to-peer programs designed to assist such populations as war veterans, law enforcement officers, emergency services, widows, hospital patients, or disaster victims, show that this approach is an effective tool for helping others cope.[54] Peer support and mentorship models are continuously being adapted by various groups for their populations based on the effectiveness of the research. In general, peer support is centered on the commonality of the cultural experience of similar events or conditions and the resilience needed to overcome adversity. WoA believes that the peer support model can be a useful tool in assisting whistleblowers problem solve and make better informed decisions while coping with the psychosocial impacts of retaliation.

Peer support is reciprocal in nature,[55] so WoAPs are whistleblowers themselves willing to engage in a "give and take" exchange. Although, the relationship is not about the mentor, the mentor gains in that they are able to give back to others and experience their own sense of posttraumatic growth because they have been able to overcome their own traumatic experiences and gain new skills. Assisting others is healing and restorative.

WoAPs know that because whistleblowing usually involves legal processes that call for privacy and confidentiality of all parties, the whistleblower can become more isolated and alienated from their management, coworkers, and other professionals. Some whistleblowers have reported that it was years later when they discovered that others were going through the same thing that they

---

[54] Defense Centers of Excellence for Psychological Health and Traumatic Brain Injury. (2011) Best Practices Identified for Peer Support Programs. Final.
[55] Castellano, C. (2012) Reciprocal peer support (RPS): a decade of not so random acts of kindness. IJEMH. Vol 14, No. 2

were, but they did not know about each other at the time. Therefore, WoAP mentors can assist in breaking down the isolation whistleblowers experience and help them establish a new network of support and resources.

WoAP mentors help a whistleblower get through the investigative process and assist them in figuring out their next steps. WoAPs can address the resilience factors that must be built, maintained, and sustained to overcome the adversity seeping throughout the whistleblower's workplace, family, and community because they have already had to deal with their own legal, financial, social, emotional and physical impacts and found the resilience skills to survive. WoAPs have experienced some facet of the disrupted sense of organizational belongingness, loss of professional meaning and purpose, feeling burdensome to family and friends, dealt with health ailments, and have had to overcome the toxic tactics used by their management. Fortunately, these challenging experiences enabled them to become stronger and more committed to justice. WoAPs are to be familiar with the concepts and tools in this guide and agree to mentor others.

WoAP Mentorship Values, Skills, and Tasks

There are several common values, skills, and tasks that are the key ingredients to making peer support effective.[56] WoA adheres to the following guiding principles for its peer support program, which includes:

Build Rapport – Finding the common ground in the whistleblowing experience and the adversity of retaliation will be the beginning of the peer relationship. Is the time and place of your meeting by phone or in person a safe and acceptable means for the mentee? Be approachable, relaxed and honest in your capabilities. Make sure the mentee feels safe and comfortable. If you do not know an answer, say so. Agree to research it with the mentee.

---

[56] Garrick, J. (2017) Peer support for whistleblowers. Federal Practitioner. July. 38-41

<u>Non-judgmental</u> – Mentors do not judge the mentee, organization, or circumstances. You can be empathetic without judging or criticizing the actions of the mentee or the wrongdoing. It is not your position to decide right or wrong or preach, but to help the mentee decide actions for him/herself. Let frustrations be ventilated. WoAPs do not adjudicate cases!

<u>Empathetic</u> – As someone who has experienced workplace hostilities or retaliation, you can relate to the circumstances and validate those emotions. You want to provide comfort and hope. Empathy is different from sympathy and involves identification, understanding, compassion, and responsiveness. Be mindful of your own experiences and how those might help the mentee.

<u>Trustworthiness</u> – A central component of the mentor/mentee relationship connection is trust. Trust can be built by explaining the WoA policy on confidentiality and by sharing your own experience. But this is not about you, so have your "elevator" version of your story ready to share. Use the tools in this guide to build your relationship and instill confidence. Do not overcommit or overpromise. Be clear and upfront about your boundaries and the mentee's.

<u>Open-end questions</u> – Gather as much information as you can about the whistleblower's situation and the retaliation that they may be experiencing. Use the *Toxic Tactics* description and review the *Risk Impacts*. Avoid questions that generate "yes" or "no" answers. Ask the mentee to describe what is going on or ask them about how they are handling the situation. Refer to the *Whistleblower Strategic Plan* to guide the conversation. Help the mentee build their own narrative impact statement and elevator speech with their desired outcomes clearly stated.

<u>Active listening</u> – Pay close attention to what is being said and find key words that identify what is going on and where in the whistleblowing process your mentee is at. This is sometimes referenced as "listening with a third ear." Restate what you heard and get clarification. Pair this technique with Reflection. Focus on the goals and outcomes that the mentee is trying to reach. Work

through any ruminations by bringing the conversation back to the end goals. Set your own parameters for the engagement so that the mentee has your undivided attention. Do not be distracted by your surroundings or other obligations.

Reflection – Mentors are mirrors. As you keep in mind to stay non-judgmental, your goal is to be able to tune in (active listening) to what is being said. Reflect it back to the mentee so that they can hear themselves "think out loud." Help the mentee identify the emotions that fit the thoughts and behaviors. What has been useful and what has been self-defeating? Use the terminology from the *Toxic Tactics* and *Risk Impacts* sections to be able to help frame what the mentee is feeling or experiencing.

Goal Setting - Use the *Whistleblower Strategic Plan* in this guide to figure out what is going on with the mentee's situation in order to set goals and determine the steps that need to be taken. Remember that the main purpose of being a mentor is to be supportive in problem solving and decision making. Prioritizing issues is an important step to goal setting. But, mentees need to know that it is OK to not feel pressured to make any decisions before they feel ready. A decision to not decide is a decision. Reducing stress is an important goal too.

A way to help guide the decision-making process is to use the SMART[57] framework:

- Specific – Keep it simple and precise in what you want to accomplish by whistleblowing and know the applicable laws. That will help shape the next steps.

- Measurable – Set up timeframes, priority areas to address, identify sources of evidence, allocate funds and other resources. Identify who might be involved, who to tell, and when to disclose information.

- Achievable – Be realistic, weigh pros and cons for what it will take to end the wrongdoing or have retaliation

---

[57] Doran, G. T. (1981). "There's a S.M.A.R.T. way to write management's goals and objectives". *Management Review*. AMA FORUM. **70** (11): 35–36.

vindicated. What are the alternatives and consequences? What will make you "whole" and who can help you reach that state?

- Relevant – Does this end the wrongdoing or the retaliation? Does it help you cope? Do not sweat the small stuff. You cannot respond to every infraction or acts of disrespect, or rudeness towards you. (You can harm your own credibility if you do.) Know the difference between bullying, harassment, retaliation or a personality conflict. And, "hunt the good stuff"[58] by also remembering to add the positive people and activities into your decision making and long-term plans.

- Timeliness – Identify limits early in the process. Track and check accomplishments. Where are you at with your goals when you are one month, six months or a year into the process? Re-evaluate your *Whistleblower Strategic Plan* based on those outcomes and course correct if necessary. It is OK to decide to move on.

Monitor Language – This can be body language if you are meeting in person, but if your mentoring sessions are by phone then listen to intonation, tone, or silences to assess emotions and reactions. If you are writing (emails, texts), there are a lot of opportunities to gather information and encourage the whistleblower to write their own narrative, which is very healing and helpful with legal documentation. Ask for feedback on what is not being said. And if something seems off, say so. Remember to monitor for signs of harm to self or others.

Humor - Maintaining a sense of humor is hard when under stressed or facing adversity but being able to keep one's sense of humor is important to resilience and happiness in life. If you can find the lighter side of a situation, it can help make it seem less awful and not as impossible to deal with. Laughter is the best medicine! But, be careful and appropriate with your humor. It can be used to help build rapport if used correctly, but ruin the bond if boundaries are crossed.

---

[58] From Army Master Resilience Training

Validate – At the end of the day, whistleblowers need to feel believed and that the retaliation that they are suffering or have experienced is harmful and life-altering. Mentees need to have their resilience affirmed. Knowing that there is a taxonomy for whistleblower retaliation and that there are classifiable impacts of that retaliation is affirming. Veterans have said that knowing others are going through the same PTSD symptoms that they are is less isolating and helps them know that it's not just them "going crazy." Having a language and a frame of reference is reassuring. It is also helpful to know what and who to be grateful for despite the negativity all around. Whistleblowers need to be encouraged, commended, and have a renewed sense of belongingness, confidence, and be able to recognize their capabilities to self-actualize. (Refer to Figure 10: Maslow's Hierarchy.)

Thank them for taking a stand against wrongdoing and for protecting people or the public from harm.

Assess for dangerousness – Although confidentiality is key, there are legal requirements to reporting suicide, homicide or child abuse. The Suicide Prevention Resource Center (SPRC) recommends the **Question, Persuade, Refer (QPR)** gatekeeper model:

- Question – Ask direct questions about suicidal thoughts or plans related to risk factors and be alert to the "IS PATH WARM" signs and symptoms identified previously.

- Persuade – Convince the whistleblower that they need to get professional help. Debunk the stigma about seeking-help or concerns about security clearances. Use a resource that is not beholden to the employer, if that is a fear. There are other options for assistance. (See Appendix E.)

- Refer – Assist them in identifying a resource for help. (See Appendix E for suggestions.) Stay with them if they are in crisis and have them contact their physician for a referral if they do not already have a mental health provider.

Keep the **National Suicide Prevention Lifeline** number with you or stored in your cellphone. You and your mentee can call the hotline together by dialing **1-800-273-8255 or chatting on the website at:** https://suicidepreventionlifeline.org**.**

If crisis is imminent call 911.

You should report any safety concerns to the WoA case manager.

Self-care – At the end of the day, you must know your limits and how to take care of yourself. Remember that a principle of peer support is that it is reciprocal in nature. If you are not feeling a sense of mutual benefit, your boundaries are not being respected, or you are being overwhelmed by the mentee, you should contact the WoA Case Manager who assigned you to your mentee. You should be engaging in relaxing and restorative activities of your own. Are you continuing to mitigate your own risk impacts? Peer support mentorship should leave you feeling fulfilled and accomplished. It should not be exhausting and draining.

NOTE: _WoAPs cannot, and do not replace an attorney in a legal matter or provide medical or mental health advice._

WoAPs can provide information on the roles and functions of EEO, EAP, OIG, OSC and the MSPB and how to navigate those systems. They can make referrals to any of those entities or other sources of additional support using WoA resources.

Using the tools in this manual, WoAPs help whistleblowers shape their stories and figure out what evidence they need or the sources to tell. If a mentee wants to go to an internal or external source, such as Congress or be interviewed by the press, the WoA tools are there to help inform those decisions.

WoA will match whistleblowers (mentees) and a WoAP mentor based on information in the WoA database as best as possible. WoAP mentors are volunteers and can refuse any match they are not

relationship is to develop a *Whistleblower Strategic Plan,* problem-solve and make decisions while building, maintaining, and sustaining resilience.

Know your limits and engage in your own self-care.

Know that you are a volunteer and are greatly appreciated by WoA.

I agree to follow the WoA principles outlined in this guide and perform the above level of support.

Name:_____

Date: _____

Appendix B

Mentee Agreement: Roles and Responsibilities of WoAP Mentee

Be respectful of your WoAP mentor. They have volunteered their time and expertise to help guide you on your journey. WoA or WoAPs are not liable for any outcomes. Respect their boundaries and the time limits that the two of you agree to at the beginning of your relationship.

I've agreed to this date & time: _____

I've agreed to this type of contact: phone/ in person

I understand the limits and boundaries of my volunteer WoAP _

I understand that WoA, its staff, and volunteers are not liable and are not providing legal, financial, or medical advice.

Use the tools in this guide to help you work through your *Whistleblower Strategic Plan* with your WoAP mentor. I will do my best to know the whistleblower laws that apply to me and will keep my activities in collecting and reporting evidence legal. I will not be insubordinate or violate any laws.

If I am overwhelmed by the risk impacts of whistleblower retaliation, I will seek legal or medical intervention. I understand that the WoAP mentor is a volunteer and not a replacement for legal or medical professional relationships. I will call the National Suicide Prevention Lifeline at 1-800-273-8255 if I feel I could hurt myself or others.

I understand the limits of confidentiality if I report intentions of suicide, homicide or child abuse.

I understand that Whistleblowers are the "First Relators of wrongdoing" and deserve respect and an environment free from harm.

Name:_____

Date: _____

Appendix C

Whistleblower Strategic Plan:

- Create your own narrative – what is the story about the wrongdoing that you want to tell?

- Create or maintain a log book or a diary of events and your thoughts. Take copious notes in meetings with dates and attendance. (This contemporaneous evidence can help your case and your attorney will ask for anything like this.) Keep track of the details.

- Have a factual timeline of occurrences. (lawyers, news reporters, and investigators will value this.)

- Keep a schedule of "due dates" if your filing or appeals are time limited. Get extensions if possible.

- Write your "elevator speech" about your situation.

- Know what resolution or outcome you seek. Remember to keep your goals SMART!

- List the proof/evidence that you have legally obtained, or an investigator should get copies (documents, reports, letters, emails, recordings, etc.). It must be more than your opinion.

- What evidence can you FOIA from the Federal Government?

- What are the restrictions (i.e.: classified, confidential, proprietary, private) you have considered about disclosing any wrongdoing?

- What are the applicable federal or state laws that address the wrongdoing identified?

- What are the regulations or policies (employee handbook) governing your organization that could impact your ability to disclose information?

- What are the applicable federal or state laws that protect you as a whistleblower? Are there court decisions that can help as legal precedence for your case?

- What forms of retaliation tactics (if any) have your suffered and documented? Refer to the *Toxic Tactics* taxonomy in this guide.

- Who do you tell? What office or agency is designed to best respond to your concerns?

- Internal?

  o List everyone who could be involved and the pros and cons of talking to them (i.e. supervisor, human resources, EO officer, union representative, coworkers, OIG, OGC, etc.)

  o Is ADR or other mediation right for you?

  o Who supports you at work? Will they sign witness statements?

  o Is your record clean? Can it handle scrutiny? Request a copy of your official personnel folder (you may have to FOIA this as well.)

  o Ask for an audit of your personnel folder and medical record to see who has accessed your files.

- External?

  o What are the pros and cons of going public?

- o If you are a government employee, do you file with EEOC, GAO, or OSC/MSPB? Do you go to Federal Court? Do you report anonymously? (This limits your whistleblower protections.)

- o If you are a civilian, do you go to DoL or Court?

- o If the wrongdoing is criminal, should you go to local law enforcement or the FBI or IRS?

- o Can you get an Order of Protection if you have proof that you have been threatened?

- o Can you send a Cease and Desist Letter?

- o Is there a professional association or a credentialing body to report to? (For example, medical errors can be reported to the Joint Commission or denied access to VA care can be reported to a VSO.)

- o Can your member of Congress or Senator support you? Is there an oversight committee with jurisdiction that would be interested?

- o Is there a state representative or local (county or city) official available to you?

- o Is there a trusted local or national press outlet or TV station to tell your story?

- o Is social media an option?

- Know how you are going to handle:

  - Legal impacts -

    - o Do you need or have an attorney?

- What are the attorney fees, areas/industry of specialization, and track record? (See Section on Hiring an Attorney)

- Do you have professional insurance that protects you in a counter lawsuit?

- If you are not able to hire an attorney and are representing yourself *pro se,* what resources and tools can you use to effectively make your own case? Do you know the applicable rules and regulations for filing and adjudicating your case? Do you have the time to do it yourself?

- What are your settlement agreement options?

- Financial Impacts –

  - Can you afford an attorney and other potential fees?

  - Are you prepared for early retirement? Job change? Career Change?

  - What are your "safety net" resources? Do you have investments?

  - Do you have a financial planner who you can consult with about your economic future?

- Social Impacts –

  - Does your family support you?

  - What can you tell family members?

  - What do you tell your children? What information is age appropriate?

42 USC § 1988(a)(b)	based on the laws found in 42 USC.
Alternative Dispute Resolution Acts of 1990, 1996, 1998	Requires that each agency have a policy that broadly makes ADR available in decision-making and that federal trial courts make ADR available to litigants.
Health Insurance Portability & Accountability Act of 1996 (HIPAA) **P.L. 104- 191**	Initiates federal standards for protecting the privacy of certain personally identifiable health information. The Department of Health and Human Services (HHS) was mandated to issue privacy rules to all related health insurers, providers, and other health organizations.
Consumer Product Safety Act **15 USC § 2087**	Protects whistleblowers who uncover consumer safety hazards and violations that can be identified to OSHA. Addresses retaliation recovery.
Dodd-Frank Wall Street Reform & Consumer Protection Act of 2010 **Commodities Exchange Act** **Securities Exchange Act**	Provides protections and rewards to original source whistleblower related to the CEA or SEA, antiretaliation provisions and relief. Civil actions can be taken if wrongfully discharged for whistleblowing. Has *qui tam* provisions
Sarbanes-Oxley Acts **(There are several sources)**	There are several related to publicly traded corporations and whistleblower identification of wrongdoing and federal court remedies.
Obstruction of Justice, Retaliation Against Whistleblowers **18 USC § 1513 (e)**	Makes it a federal felony to harm a whistleblower's livelihood in relation to federal law enforcement disclosures.
Environmental Whistleblower Protections	Within 30 days, a whistleblower must file a DoL claim for any retaliation remedies.

(There are several sources depending on air, water, or land contamination)	
Federal Acquisition Regulations (FAR) **48 CFR**	Protects federal contract whistleblowers from retaliation and mandates compliance programs and ethics training.
DoD Contract Fraud Retaliation **10 USC § 2409**	Prohibits reprisal against DoD or NASA whistleblowers who disclose contract or grant mismanagement or waste of funds to the OIG. Allows cases to go to federal court after all administrative remedies are exhausted for remuneration.
IRS Payment for Detection of Fraud and Underpayment of Taxes	Rewards IRS whistleblowers with 10-30% of recovered funds and creates an office. Does <u>not</u> protect employees.
Fair Labor Standards Act of 1938	Allows employees to file FLSA claims in federal court for retaliation or with the DoL within 2 years of adverse action.
National Labor Relations Act of 1935 **29 USC §§ 151-16**	Permits unions and collective bargaining. Also, protects employees not affiliated with a union to engage in concerted, protected activity by which one or more employees seek to improve the terms and conditions of employment of all employees, such as complaints about wages and benefits.
Dr. Chris Kirkpatrick Whistleblower Protection Act of 2017 **P.L. 115-73**	Directs federal agencies (excluding intelligence) to prioritize employee transfer request if MSPB grants a stay when OSC determines prohibited personnel practice; or if the employee is on probation and seeks corrective action. Prohibits accessing medical

	records of another employee or applicant (VA must have a specific plan) and authorizes disciplinary action against supervisors for retaliation against whistleblowers.
	Agencies must report employee suicides to the OSC, train supervisors on responding to complaints alleging whistleblower protections violations, provide information regarding those protections to all and newly hired employees, inform employees about OSC
	GAO shall assess the reporting, staffing, accountability, and chain of command structure of the VA police officers at VA medical centers

Appendix E

Whistleblower Resource Guide

These are government and nonprofit resources that might be useful to a whistleblower or watchdog developing their own strategic plan. This listing is not comprehensive and does not constitute an endorsement of any products or services and should be used at your own discretion. There are a host of law firms, financial advisors, clinicians and other professionals that can be researched beyond this scope. Consider comparing services and cost estimates.

Employment Searches and Tools

These are organizations that can help you find a new job or see if the company/organization you are considering as an employer has good reviews and is rated as an organization of choice. (Also see Federal Government Resources, OPM/USAJOBS, for federal job information and SBA for business ownership)

Gallup Strengths Center
(Assess your unique strengths)
https://www.gallupstrengthscenter.com/

Glassdoor
(Organization of choice and job searches)
https://www.glassdoor.com/index.htm

Indeed
(Job Searches)
https://www.indeed.com/

Lean In
(Find a Mentor or a Circle)
https://leanin.org/

Linkedin
(Job searches and profiles)
https://www.linkedin.com/jobs/

Monster
(Job searches)
https://www.monster.com/

Organization Development Network
(Performance and Personnel Management for Success)
http://www.odnetwork.org/?page=WhatIsOD
651-379-7292

SCORE Association
(Information and Mentors for starting and owning a small business)
https://www.score.org/
800-634-0245

Federal Government Resources

These are the federal agencies that provide oversight and support services for whistleblowers. Each federal agency has its own OIG that should be contacted to report waste, fraud, or abuse within that agency. Check agency website if not listed in the WoA Resource Guide

Consumer Financial Protection Bureau
(Assistance with Financial Fraud Against Individuals)
https://www.consumerfinance.gov/
855-411-2372

Commodity and Futures Trading Commission
(Assistance with Business Fraud)
https://www.whistleblower.gov/default.aspx

Department of Defense (DoD)
(There are several sources for DoD, the following are limited to reporting to the DoD OIG, National Guard Employment issues, and security clearance concerns)

Computer/Electronic Accommodations Program Technology and Evaluation Center (CAPTEC)
(Provides ALL disabled federal employees with reasonable accommodation support)
http://www.cap.mil/Customers/CAPTEC.aspx
cap.captec@mail.mil
703- 693-5160

Employer Support for the Guard and Reserves (ESGR)
http://esgr.mil/USERRA/What-is-USERRA
800-336-4590, Option 1
(Also see Department of Labor – USERRA)

DoD Inspector General
http://www.dodig.mil/
800-424-9098 (Toll-Free)
703-604-8799 (Commercial)
664-8799 (DSN)

Defense Security Clearance Information and Mental Health
http://www.realwarriors.net/active/treatment/clearance.php

Department of Health and Human Services
(Report Medicare/Medicaid fraud, child support enforcement, consumer alerts and contracts/grants fraud. HHS works with state False Claims Act cases.)
https://oig.hhs.gov/fraud/

Office For Civil Rights
(Report HIPAA or other privacy violations)
https://www.hhs.gov/ocr/complaints/index.html
800-368-1019

Financial Planning Services

These nonprofit resources can provide a review of your financial situation, retirement goals and investment strategy with consideration of your employment situation. There are numerous private investment firms and advisors to choose from.

National Foundation for Credit Counseling
https://www.nfcc.org/
800-388-2227

Serving Those Who Serve
(specializing in government employees and benefits)
http://stwserve.com/
301-216-1167
1-800-437-STWS (7897)

Mental Health Providers

These resources will have mental health educational information and referrals for treatment providers or crisis services. There are several hotlines that provide support every day of the year.

American Academy of Experts in Traumatic Stress (AAETS)
http://www.aaets.org
631-543-2217

American Association of Suicidology (AAS)
http://www.suicidology.org
202-237-2280

American Psychiatric Association (APA)
https://www.psychiatry.org/
703- 907-7300

American Psychological Association (APA)
http://locator.apa.org/
800-373-2722

APA -American Psychology – Law Society
http://www.apadivisions.org/division-41/index.aspx

Anxiety and Depression Association of America
http://www.adaa.org
240-485-1001

Association for Behavioral and Cognitive Therapies
http://www.abct.org
212-647-1890

EMDR Institute
Eye Movement Desensitization and Reprocessing therapy locator
http://www.emdr.com
831-761-1040

International Critical Incident Stress Foundation (ICISF)
http://www.icisf.org
410-750-9600

International Society for Traumatic Stress Studies (ISTSS)
http://www.istss.org
847-480-9028

National Association of Social Workers (NASW)
http://socialworkers.org/
800-742-4089

National Alliance on Mental Illness (NAMI)
http://nami.org
703-524-9094

Rape, Abuse, & Incest National Network (RAINN)
http://www.rainn.org
202-544-1034
> **National Sexual Assault Hotline**
> **1-800-656-4673**

202-265-PEER (7337)
Project On Government Oversight (POGO)
http://www.pogo.org/
202-347-1122

Protect Our Defenders (military sexual trauma)
www.protectourdefenders.com

The Rutherford Institute
www.rutherford.org
434-978-3888

Whistleblower Aid
www.whistlebloweraid.org

Whistleblowers International Network
https://whistleblowingnetwork.org/

Whistleblower Support Fund
https://whistleblowing.us/
301-953-7353

Workplace Bullying Institute
www.workplacebullying.org

Whistleblowers of America

601 Pennsylvania Ave, NW, South Tower, Suite 900, Washington, DC 20004

Web: www.whistleblowersofamerica.org   Twitter: @whistleP2P

Made in the USA
San Bernardino, CA
29 April 2018